To: Jani + Arlo,

Aren't Dogs the Greatest?!

Rudy + I hope you like our story!

♡ Corinne + Rudy

For
Laura

Without the generosity of others, this book would not have been possible. The author gratefully acknowledges assistance from the Francis H. Zimbeaux trust. Zimbeaux was a successful Utah artist who loved animals and nature and who wished to support emerging artists. To view his artwork, go to www.zimbeaux.com.

I would also like to thank my friends, family, and my parents, Janice and Joseph Humphrey, for their unwavering encouragement and support of this project.

Thanks also to my editor, Julie Romeis, and the rest of the stellar Chronicle staff for helping me create such a fun book.

Library of Congress Cataloging-in-Publication Data available.
ISBN 978-0-8118-7783-1

Book design by Izzy Langridge.
Typeset in Duckface and Avenir.

Manufactured by by Toppan Leefung, Da Ling Shan Town, Dongguan, China, in January 2011.

10 9 8 7 6 5 4 3 2 1

This product conforms to CPSIA 2008.

Chronicle Books LLC
680 Second Street, San Francisco, California 94107

www.chroniclekids.com

Shoot
for the
MOON!

Lessons on Life from a Dog Named Rudy

Corinne Humphrey

chronicle books · san francisco

It doesn't matter what kind of dog you are...

you can create the life you want.

Find a

HERO.

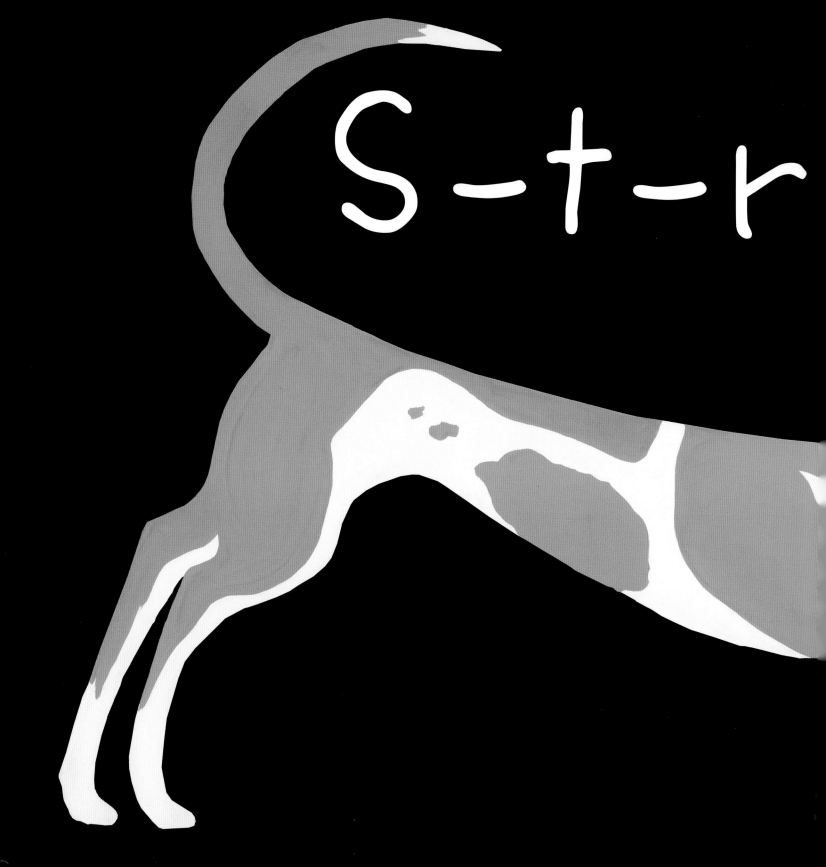

-e-t-c-h yourself,

take the
leap,

and shoot for the

MOON!

Don't be
afraid of
your shadow.

Find a
balance...

When you
follow your
guiding
STAR,

you will find
happiness
wherever
you are!

Rudy & Corinne

In 2005, I left a 25-year career as an international flight attendant to seek a more creative, balanced life. The best thing about "coming in for a final landing" was that I could finally take those paintings classes I'd always talked about, and I could get a dog.

I made numerous visits to the Friends of Animals Utah adoption center, Furburbia, looking for a four-legged companion that "spoke" to me. Rudy (formerly known as Bob) was skinny, scarred, and becoming kennel aggressive after three years bouncing in and out of shelters and foster homes. He was not my first, second, or third choice, but the knowledgeable staff convinced me to "just take him outside, give him a chance—he's our favorite." After a short stroll, we made our way to a nearby park bench. Rudy sighed, dropped his head, and leaned his whole body against my leg, fixing me with a deep, soulful gaze that seemed filled with both hope and despair at the same time. I was hooked. Any relationship takes work, and with lots of love and the help of trainers, neighbors, and dog-loving friends, we've overcome many past issues.

When I began painting Rudy, I'd often find myself giggling while sitting at the easel, and I slowly gained confidence with my art. Most of my paintings evolve from life lessons that I learn from Rudy, and his positive messages have appealed to people of all ages.

This book was originally self-published in 2007 as *The Tao of Rudy*. It earned Independent Publisher's Bronze "IPPY"

Award for Most Outstanding Book Design and also received Honorable Mention in *ForeWord Reviews* magazine's Book of the Year Awards.

Rudy hasn't forgotten what it's like to be homeless. He's donating 10 percent of net proceeds to Friends of Animals Utah (www.foautah.org) so more dogs can find good homes, too.